GROWN SWEET HOME #3

ABDO
Spotlight

DARK HORSE COMICS

PopCap

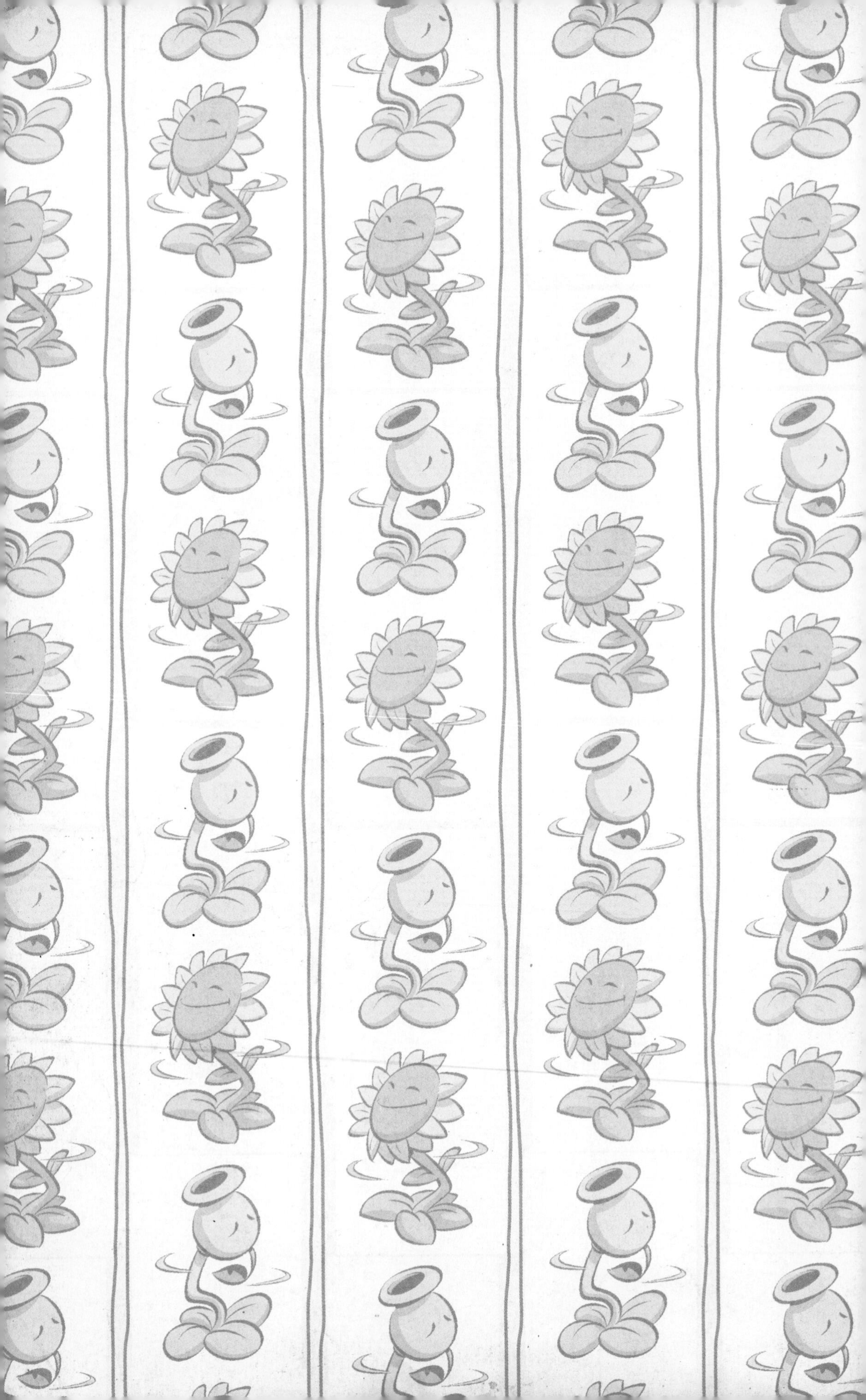

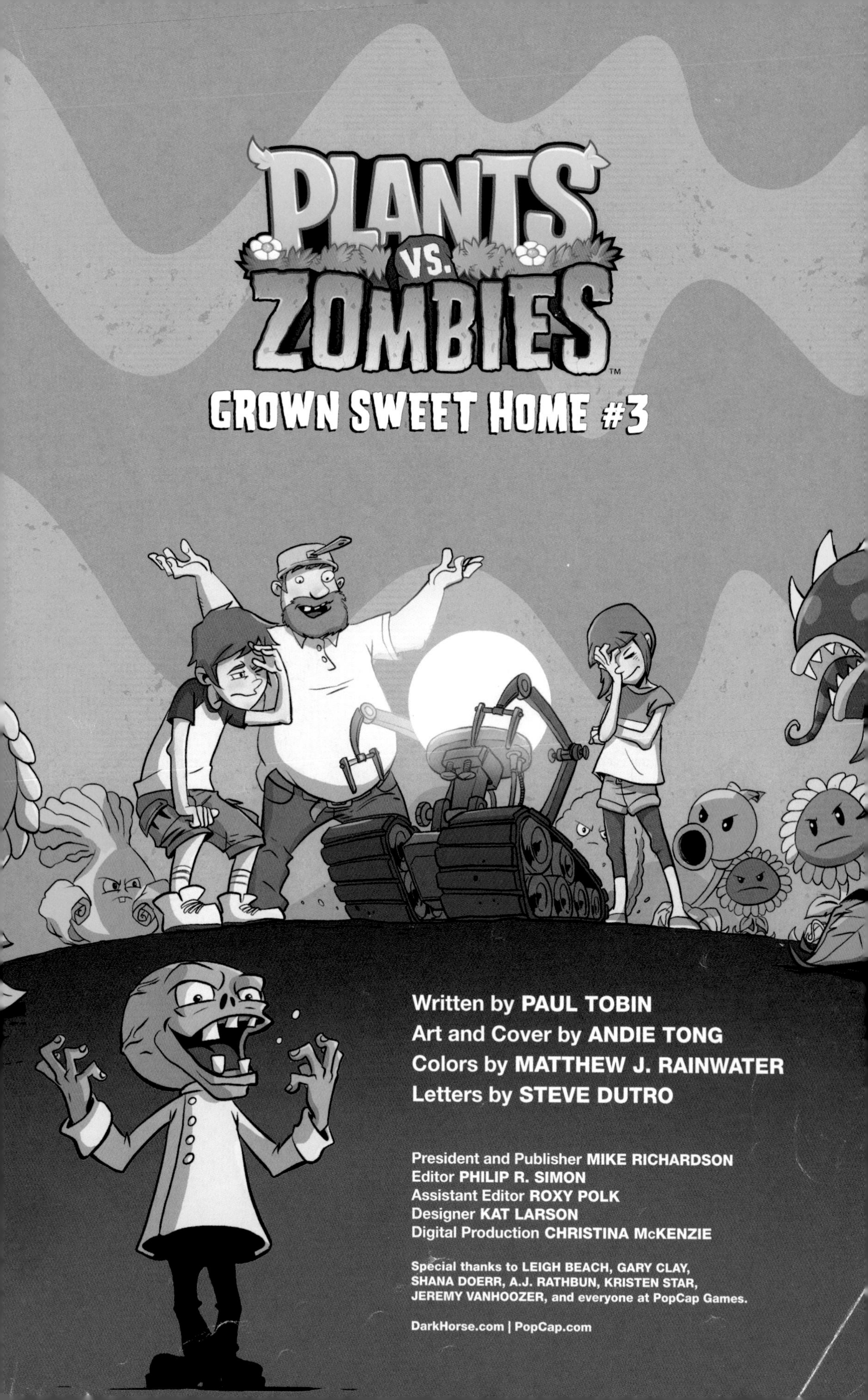

PLANTS VS. ZOMBIES™

GROWN SWEET HOME #3

Written by **PAUL TOBIN**
Art and Cover by **ANDIE TONG**
Colors by **MATTHEW J. RAINWATER**
Letters by **STEVE DUTRO**

President and Publisher **MIKE RICHARDSON**
Editor **PHILIP R. SIMON**
Assistant Editor **ROXY POLK**
Designer **KAT LARSON**
Digital Production **CHRISTINA McKENZIE**

Special thanks to **LEIGH BEACH, GARY CLAY, SHANA DOERR, A.J. RATHBUN, KRISTEN STAR, JEREMY VANHOOZER,** and everyone at **PopCap Games.**

DarkHorse.com | PopCap.com

ABDOPUBLISHING.COM

Reinforced library bound edition published in 2017 by Spotlight, a division of ABDO,
PO Box 398166, Minneapolis, Minnesota 55439. Spotlight produces high-quality
reinforced library bound editions for schools and libraries.
Published by agreement with Dark Horse Comics.

Printed in the United States of America, North Mankato, Minnesota.
042016
092016

THIS BOOK CONTAINS
RECYCLED MATERIALS

PopCap

Originally issued as Plants vs. Zombies #6: Grown Sweet Home Part 3
by Dark Horse Comics in 2015.

PUBLISHER'S CATALOGING IN PUBLICATION DATA

Names: Tobin, Paul, author. | Tong, Andie ; Rainwater, Matthew J., illustrators.
Title: Grown sweet home / by Paul Tobin ; illustrated by Andie Tong and Matthew J.
   Rainwater.
Description: Minneapolis, MN : Spotlight, [2017] | Series: Plants vs. zombies
Summary: Patrice, Nate, and Crazy Dave give the plants advice on how to act human
   when they move into Crazy Dave's mansion, but they are unaware that Zomboss is
   spying on them so he can teach the zombies how to act human.
Identifiers: LCCN 2016934736 | ISBN 9781614795377 (v.1 : lib. bdg.) | ISBN
   9781614795384 (v.2 : lib. bdg.) | ISBN 9781614795391 (v.3 : lib. bdg.)
Subjects: LCSH: Plants--Juvenile fiction. | Zombies--Juvenile fiction. | Adventure and
   adventurers--Juvenile fiction. | Comic books, strips, etc.--Juvenile fiction. | Graphic
   novels--Juvenile fiction.
Classification: DDC 741.5--dc23
LC record available at http://lccn.loc.gov/2016934736

Spotlight

A Division of ABDO
abdopublishing.com

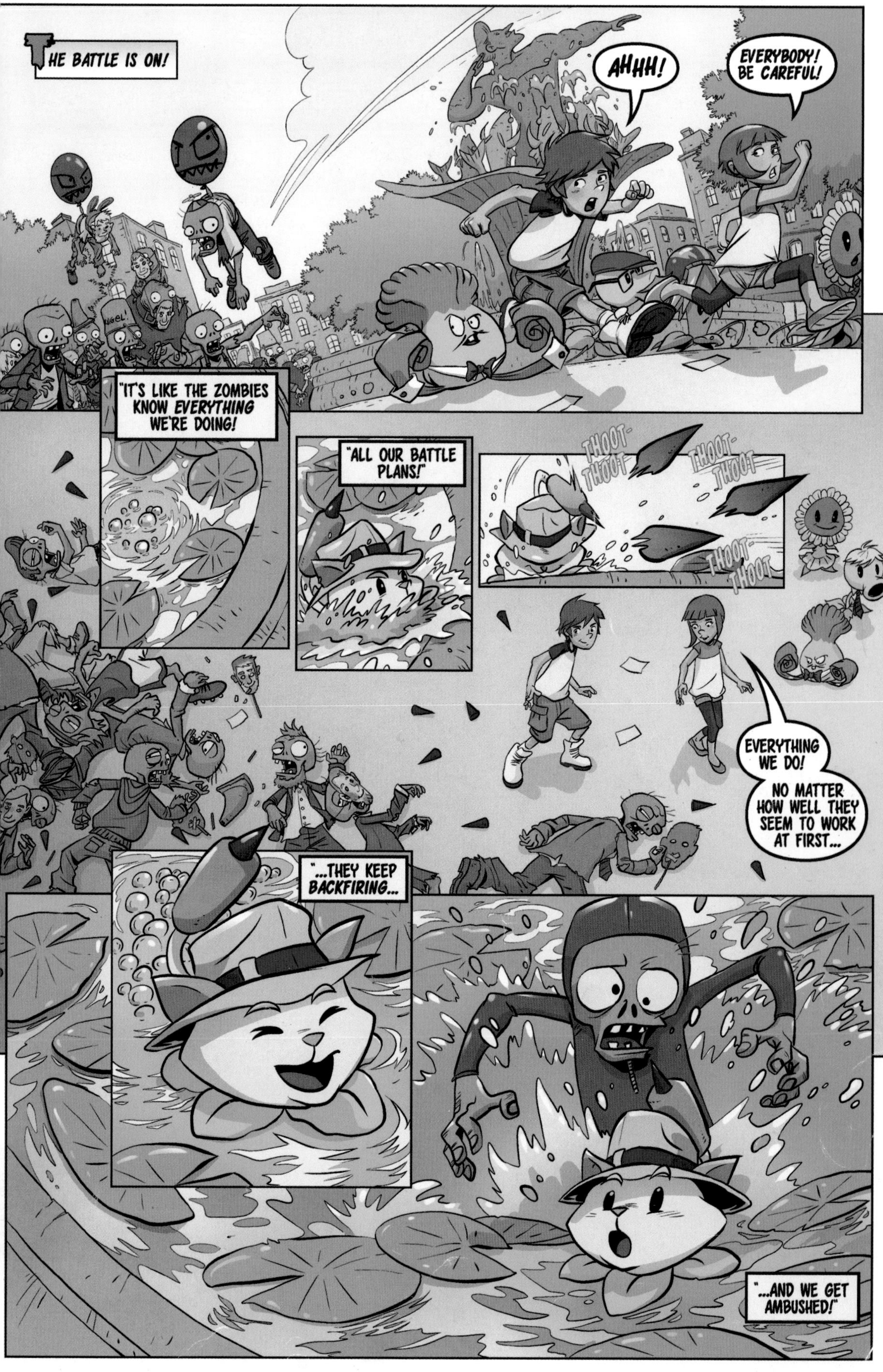
THE BATTLE IS ON!
AHHH!
EVERYBODY! BE CAREFUL!
"IT'S LIKE THE ZOMBIES KNOW EVERYTHING WE'RE DOING!
"ALL OUR BATTLE PLANS!"
THOOT-THOOT
THOOT-THOOT
THOOT-THOOT
EVERYTHING WE DO!
NO MATTER HOW WELL THEY SEEM TO WORK AT FIRST...
"...THEY KEEP BACKFIRING...
"...AND WE GET AMBUSHED!"

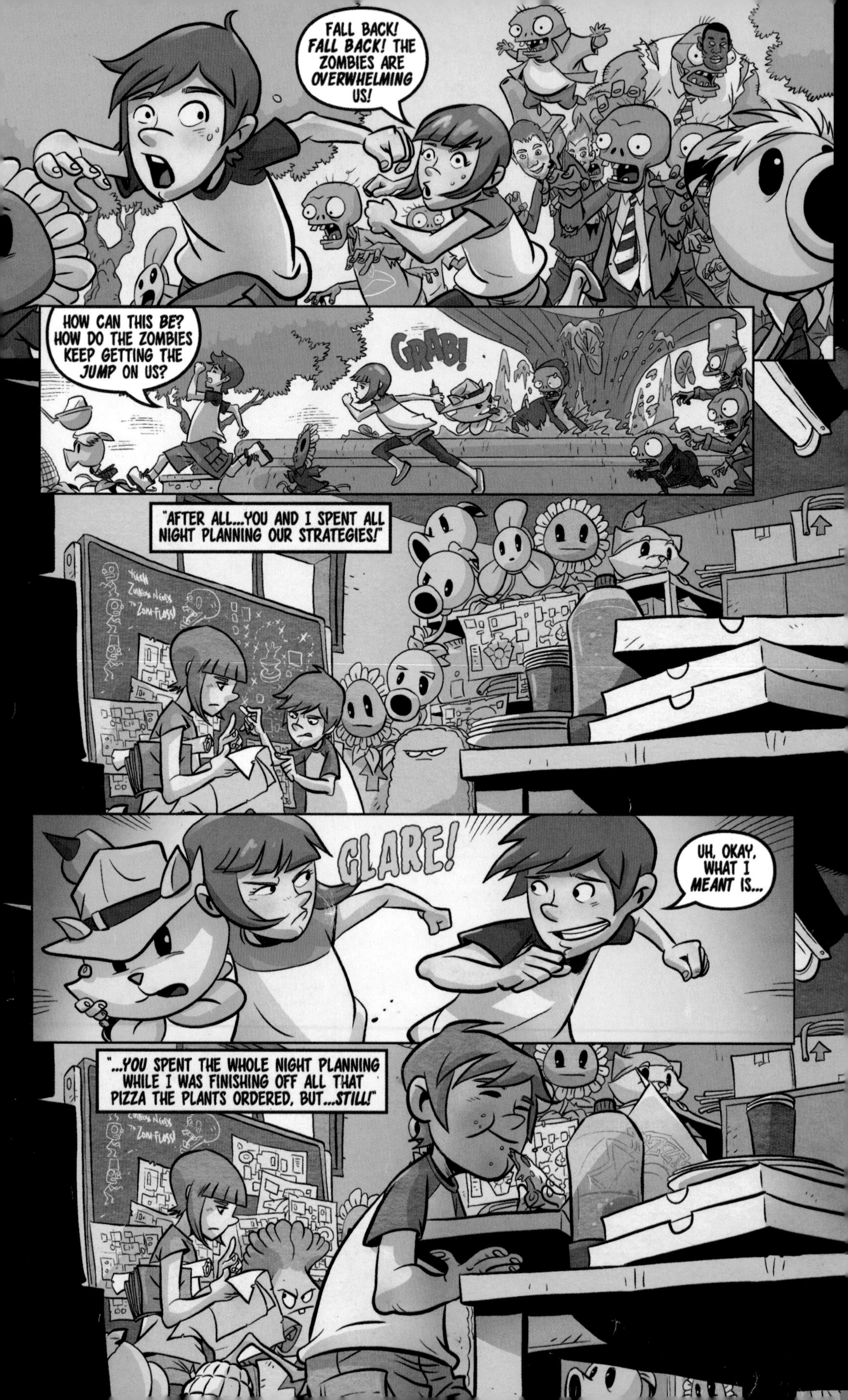

FALL BACK! FALL BACK! THE ZOMBIES ARE OVERWHELMING US!
HOW CAN THIS BE? HOW DO THE ZOMBIES KEEP GETTING THE JUMP ON US?
GRAB!
"AFTER ALL...YOU AND I SPENT ALL NIGHT PLANNING OUR STRATEGIES!"
GLARE!
UH, OKAY, WHAT I MEANT IS...
"...YOU SPENT THE WHOLE NIGHT PLANNING WHILE I WAS FINISHING OFF ALL THAT PIZZA THE PLANTS ORDERED, BUT...STILL!"

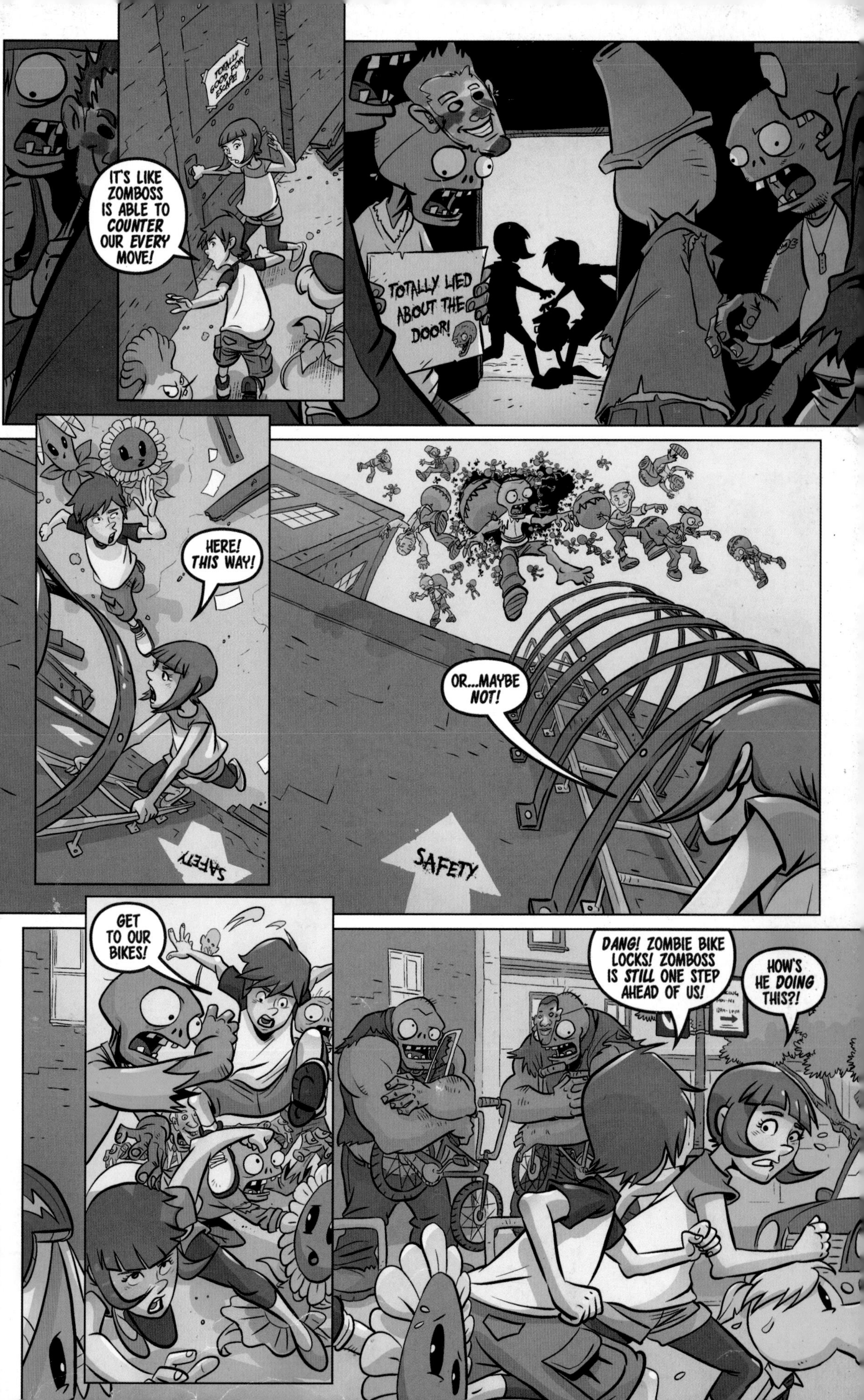
TOTALLY GOOD FOR ESCAPE!
IT'S LIKE ZOMBOSS IS ABLE TO COUNTER OUR EVERY MOVE!
TOTALLY LIED ABOUT THE DOOR!
HERE! THIS WAY!
SAFETY
OR...MAYBE NOT!
SAFETY
GET TO OUR BIKES!
DANG! ZOMBIE BIKE LOCKS! ZOMBOSS IS STILL ONE STEP AHEAD OF US!
HOW'S HE DOING THIS?!

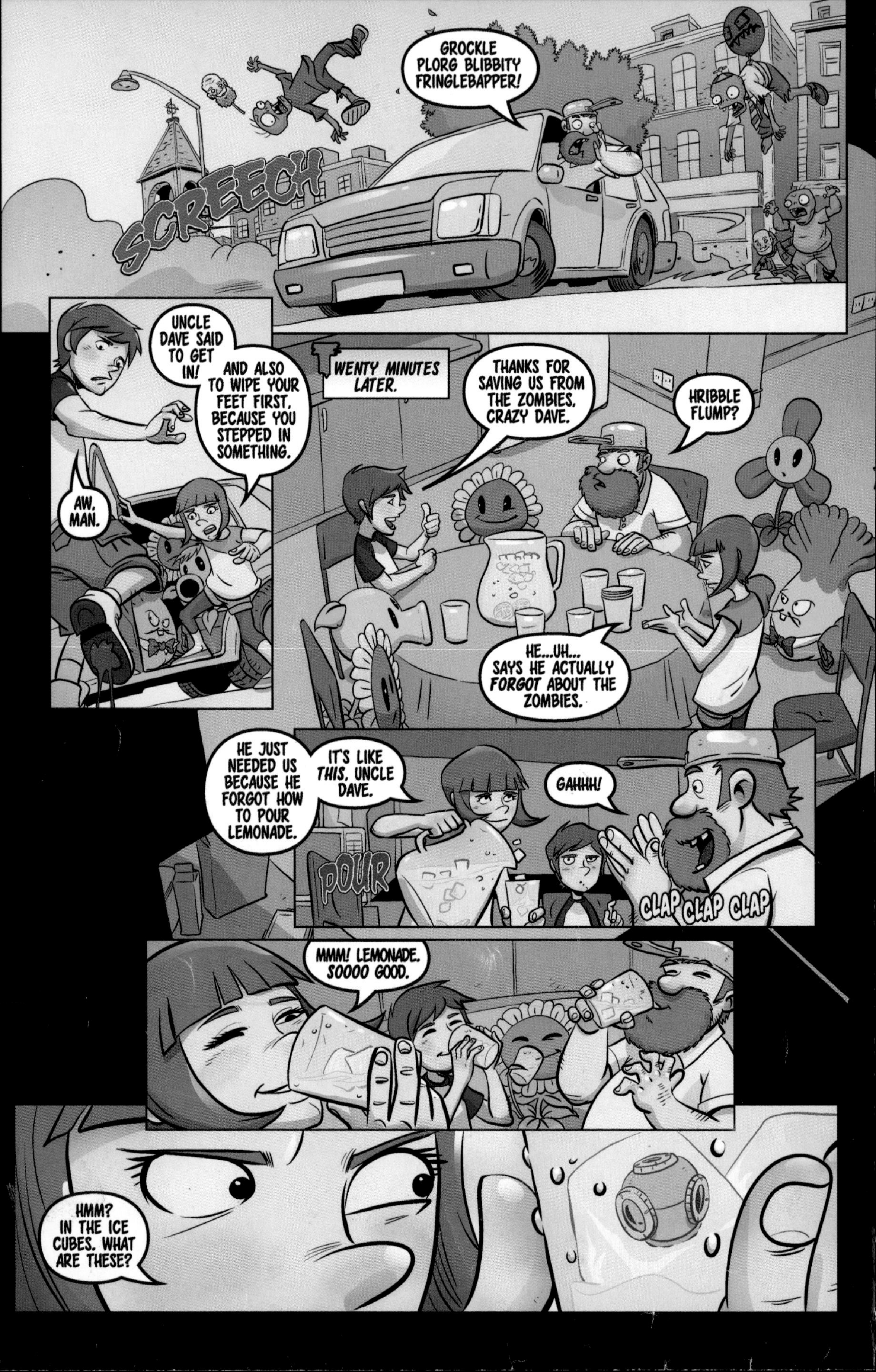
GROCKLE PLORG BLIBBITY FRINGLEBAPPER!
SCREECH
UNCLE DAVE SAID TO GET IN!
AND ALSO TO WIPE YOUR FEET FIRST, BECAUSE YOU STEPPED IN SOMETHING.
AW, MAN.
TWENTY MINUTES LATER.
THANKS FOR SAVING US FROM THE ZOMBIES, CRAZY DAVE.
HRIBBLE FLUMP?
HE...UH... SAYS HE ACTUALLY FORGOT ABOUT THE ZOMBIES.
HE JUST NEEDED US BECAUSE HE FORGOT HOW TO POUR LEMONADE.
IT'S LIKE THIS, UNCLE DAVE.
GAHHH!
POUR
CLAP CLAP CLAP
MMM! LEMONADE. SOOOO GOOD.
HMM? IN THE ICE CUBES. WHAT ARE THESE?

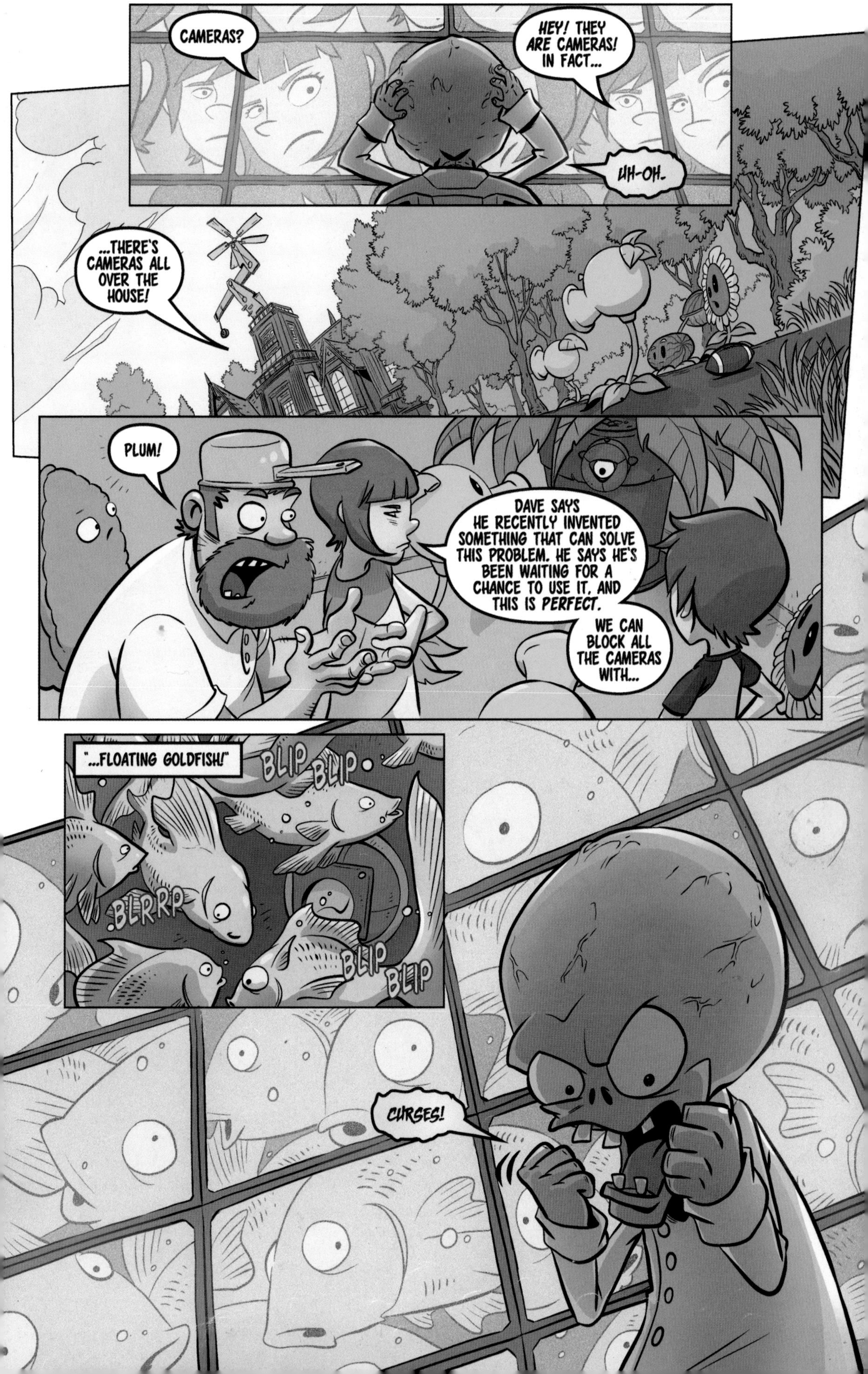
CAMERAS?
HEY! THEY ARE CAMERAS! IN FACT...
UH-OH.
...THERE'S CAMERAS ALL OVER THE HOUSE!
PLUM!
DAVE SAYS HE RECENTLY INVENTED SOMETHING THAT CAN SOLVE THIS PROBLEM. HE SAYS HE'S BEEN WAITING FOR A CHANCE TO USE IT, AND THIS IS PERFECT.
WE CAN BLOCK ALL THE CAMERAS WITH...
"...FLOATING GOLDFISH!"
BLIP BLIP
BLRRP
BLIP BLIP
CURSES!

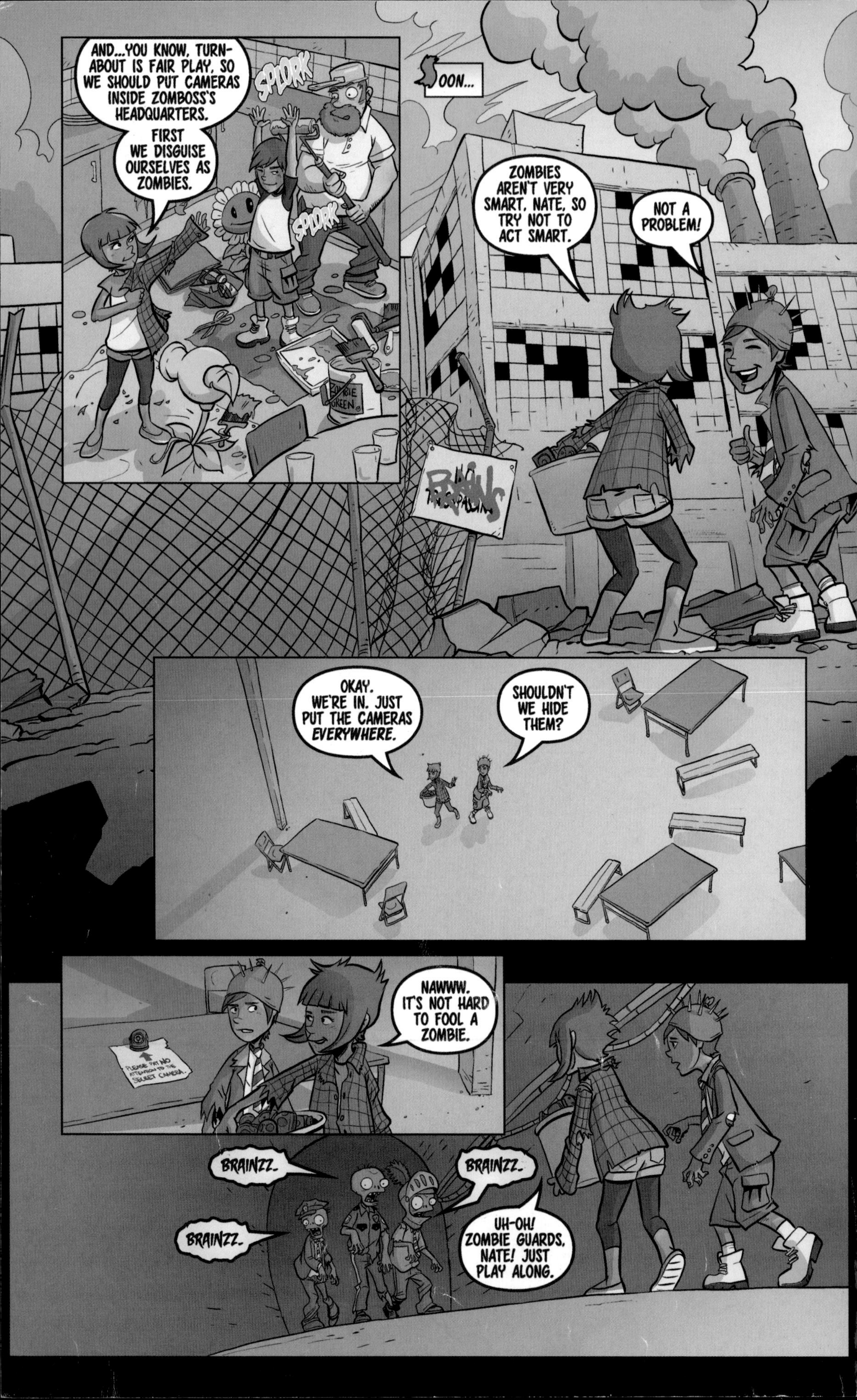
AND...YOU KNOW, TURN-ABOUT IS FAIR PLAY, SO WE SHOULD PUT CAMERAS INSIDE ZOMBOSS'S HEADQUARTERS.
FIRST WE DISGUISE OURSELVES AS ZOMBIES.
SPLORK
SPLORK
ZOMBIE GREEN
SOON...
ZOMBIES AREN'T VERY SMART, NATE, SO TRY NOT TO ACT SMART.
NOT A PROBLEM!
BRAINS
OKAY. WE'RE IN. JUST PUT THE CAMERAS *EVERYWHERE.*
SHOULDN'T WE HIDE THEM?
PLEASE PAY NO ATTENTION TO THE SECRET CAMERA.
NAWWW. IT'S NOT HARD TO FOOL A ZOMBIE.
BRAINZZ.
BRAINZZ.
BRAINZZ.
UH-OH! ZOMBIE GUARDS, NATE! JUST PLAY ALONG.

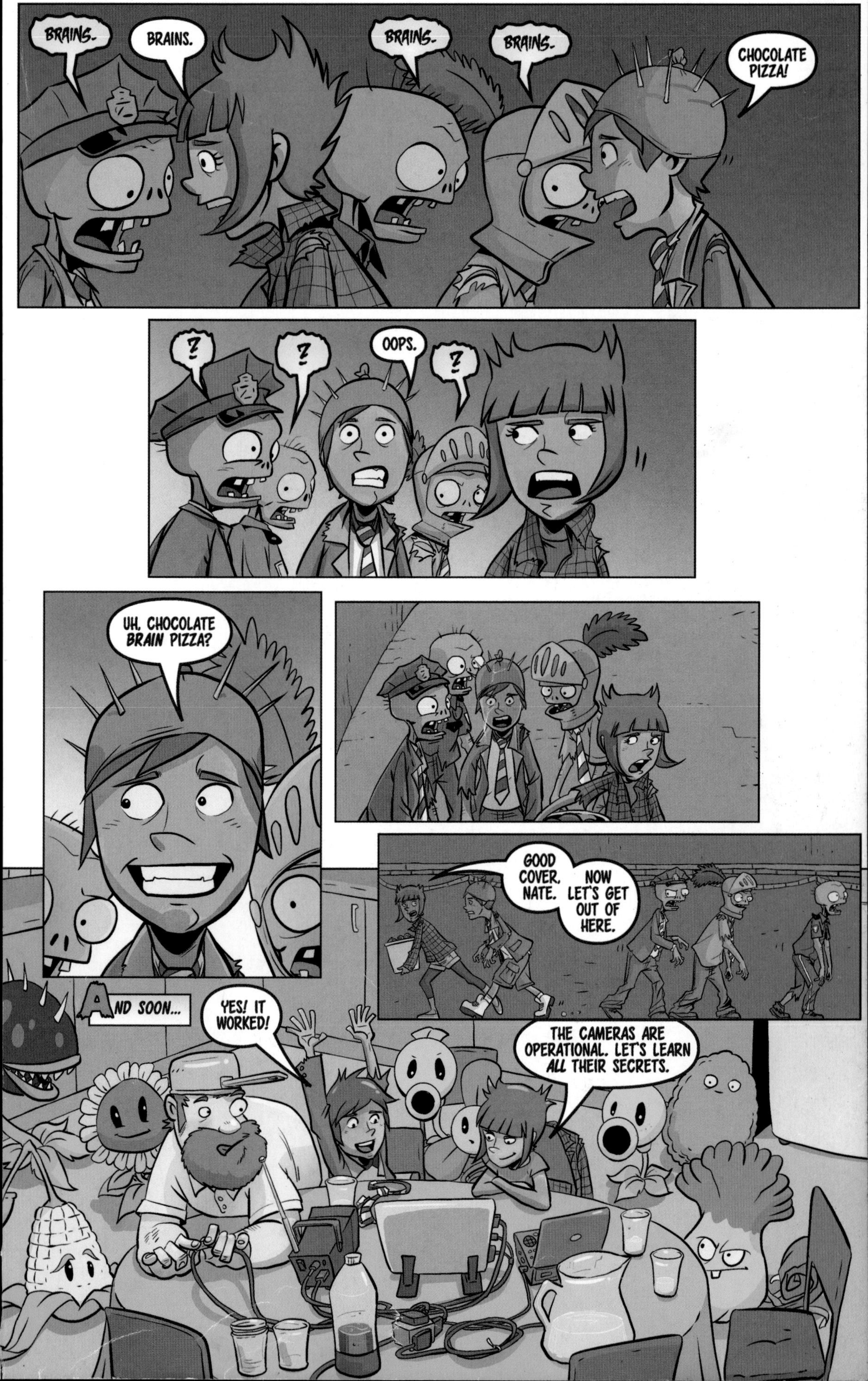

BRAINS.
BRAINS.
BRAINS.
BRAINS.
CHOCOLATE PIZZA!
?
?
OOPS.
?
UH, CHOCOLATE BRAIN PIZZA?
GOOD COVER, NATE.
NOW LET'S GET OUT OF HERE.
AND SOON...
YES! IT WORKED!
THE CAMERAS ARE OPERATIONAL. LET'S LEARN ALL THEIR SECRETS.

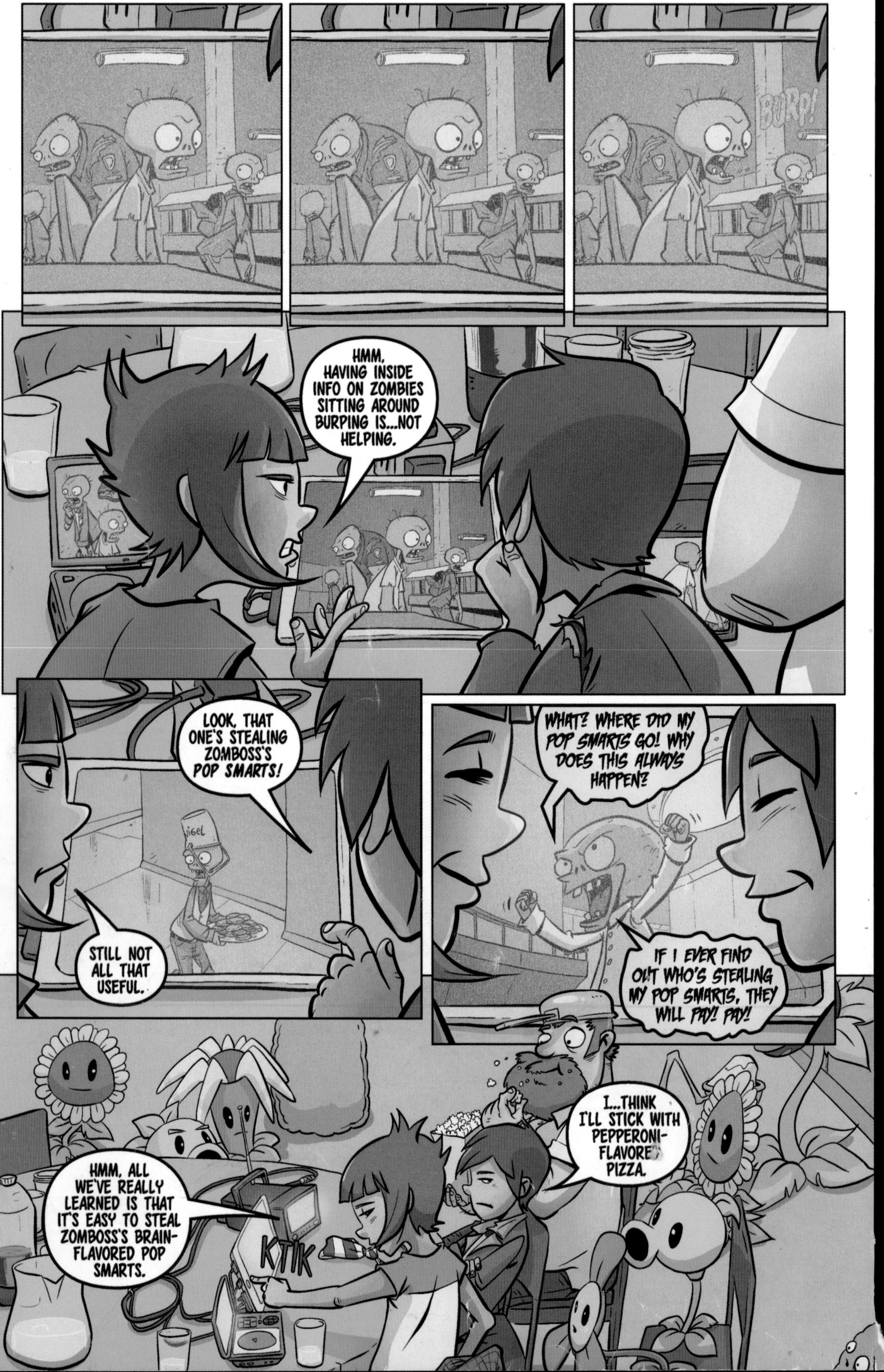
BURP!
HMM, HAVING INSIDE INFO ON ZOMBIES SITTING AROUND BURPING IS...NOT HELPING.
LOOK, THAT ONE'S STEALING ZOMBOSS'S POP SMARTS!
STILL NOT ALL THAT USEFUL.
WHAT? WHERE DID MY POP SMARTS GO! WHY DOES THIS ALWAYS HAPPEN?
IF I EVER FIND OUT WHO'S STEALING MY POP SMARTS, THEY WILL PAY! PAY!
HMM, ALL WE'VE REALLY LEARNED IS THAT IT'S EASY TO STEAL ZOMBOSS'S BRAIN-FLAVORED POP SMARTS.
KTIK
I...THINK I'LL STICK WITH PEPPERONI-FLAVORED PIZZA.

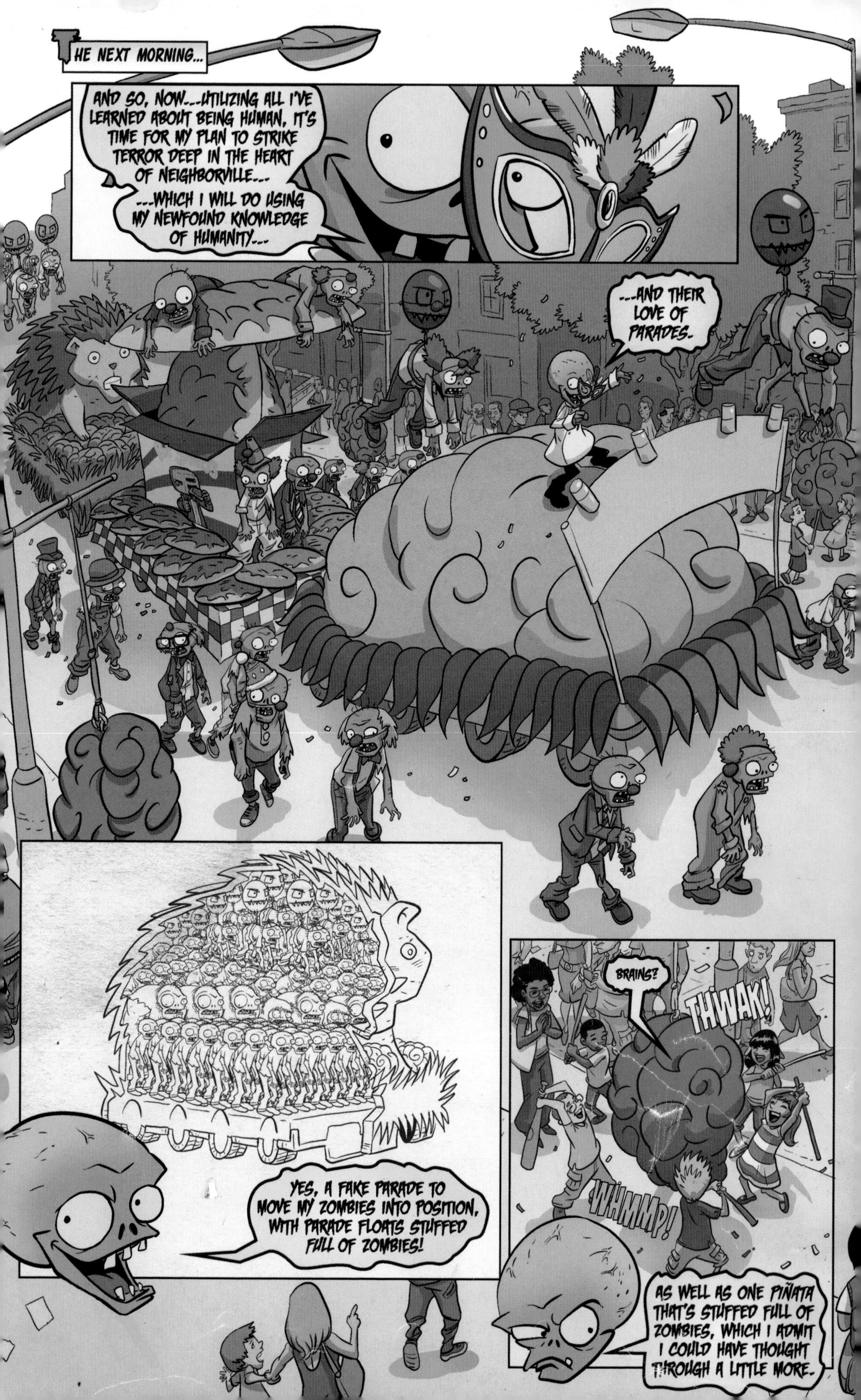
THE NEXT MORNING...
AND SO, NOW...UTILIZING ALL I'VE LEARNED ABOUT BEING HUMAN, IT'S TIME FOR MY PLAN TO STRIKE TERROR DEEP IN THE HEART OF NEIGHBORVILLE...
...WHICH I WILL DO USING MY NEWFOUND KNOWLEDGE OF HUMANITY...
...AND THEIR LOVE OF PARADES.
YES, A FAKE PARADE TO MOVE MY ZOMBIES INTO POSITION, WITH PARADE FLOATS STUFFED FULL OF ZOMBIES!
BRAINS?
THWAK!
WHMMP!
AS WELL AS ONE PIÑATA THAT'S STUFFED FULL OF ZOMBIES, WHICH I ADMIT I COULD HAVE THOUGHT THROUGH A LITTLE MORE.

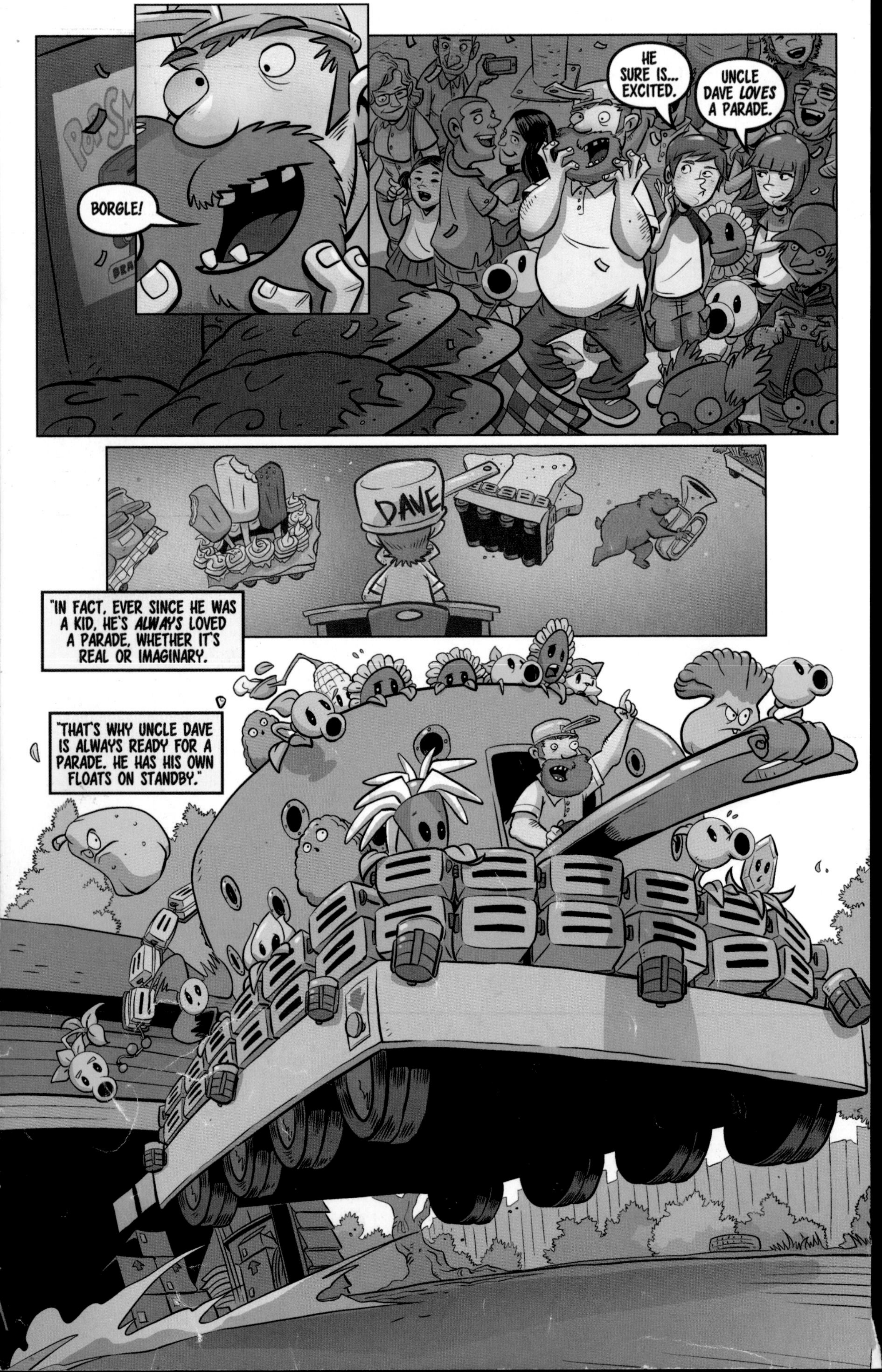
BORGLE!
HE SURE IS... EXCITED.
UNCLE DAVE *LOVES* A PARADE.
DAVE
"IN FACT, EVER SINCE HE WAS A KID, HE'S *ALWAYS* LOVED A PARADE, WHETHER IT'S REAL OR IMAGINARY.
"THAT'S WHY UNCLE DAVE IS ALWAYS READY FOR A PARADE. HE HAS HIS OWN FLOATS ON STANDBY."

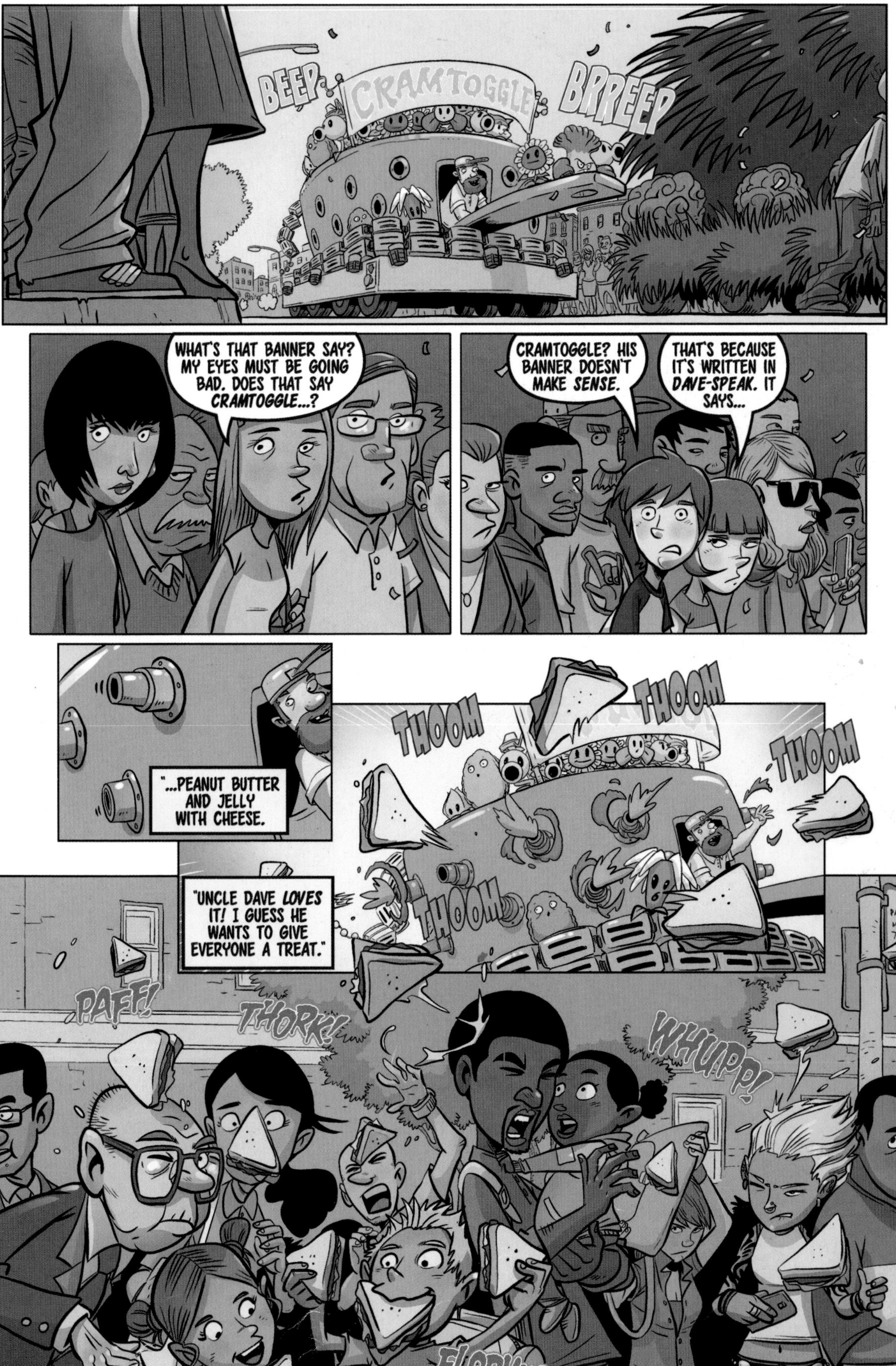
BEEP
CRAMTOGGLE
BRREEP
WHAT'S THAT BANNER SAY? MY EYES MUST BE GOING BAD. DOES THAT SAY CRAMTOGGLE...?
CRAMTOGGLE? HIS BANNER DOESN'T MAKE SENSE.
THAT'S BECAUSE IT'S WRITTEN IN DAVE-SPEAK. IT SAYS...
"...PEANUT BUTTER AND JELLY WITH CHEESE.
THOOM
THOOM
THOOM
"UNCLE DAVE LOVES IT! I GUESS HE WANTS TO GIVE EVERYONE A TREAT."
THOOM
PAFF!
THORK!
WHUPP!
FLORNK!

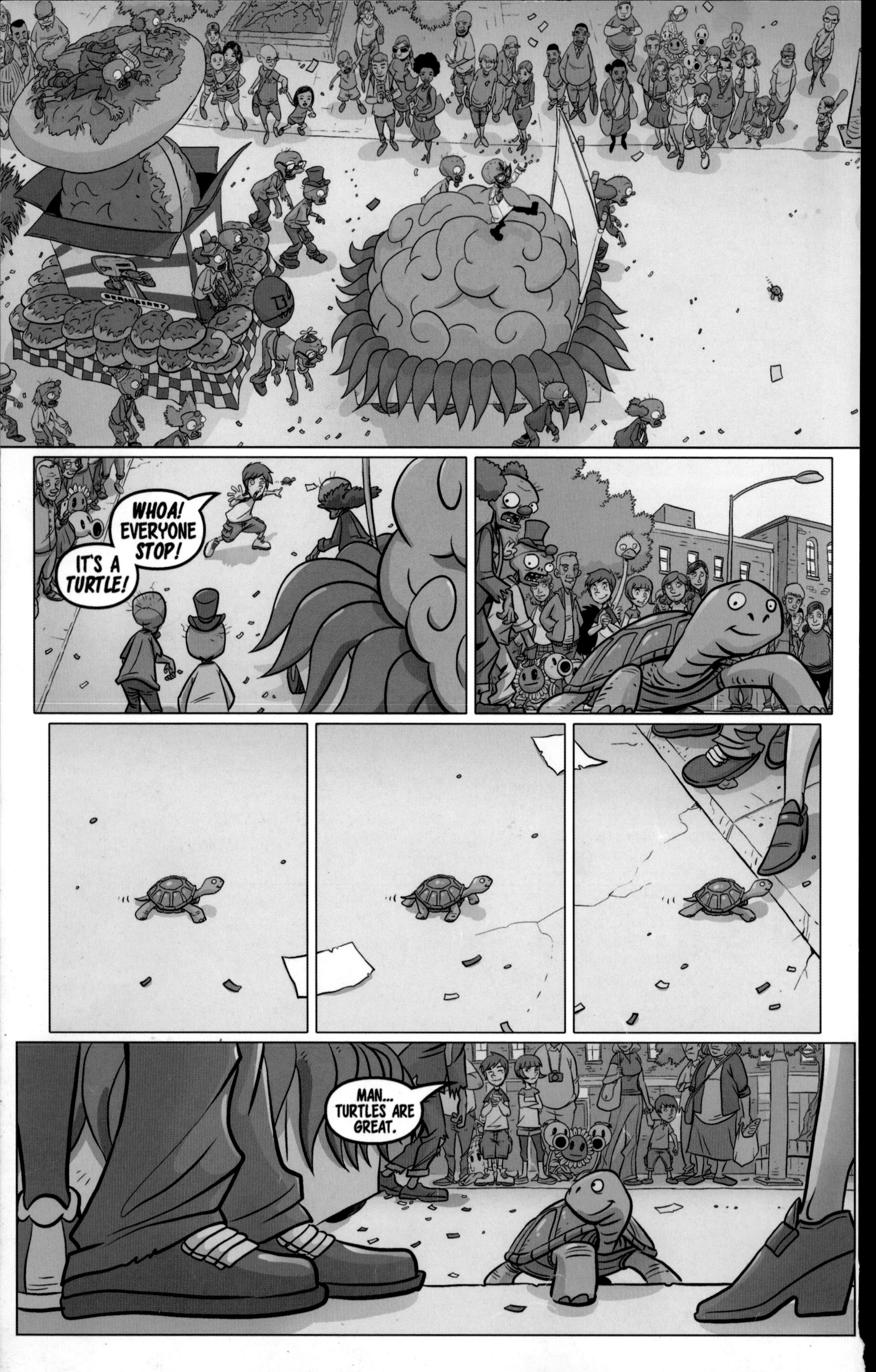
WHOA! EVERYONE STOP!
IT'S A TURTLE!
MAN... TURTLES ARE GREAT.

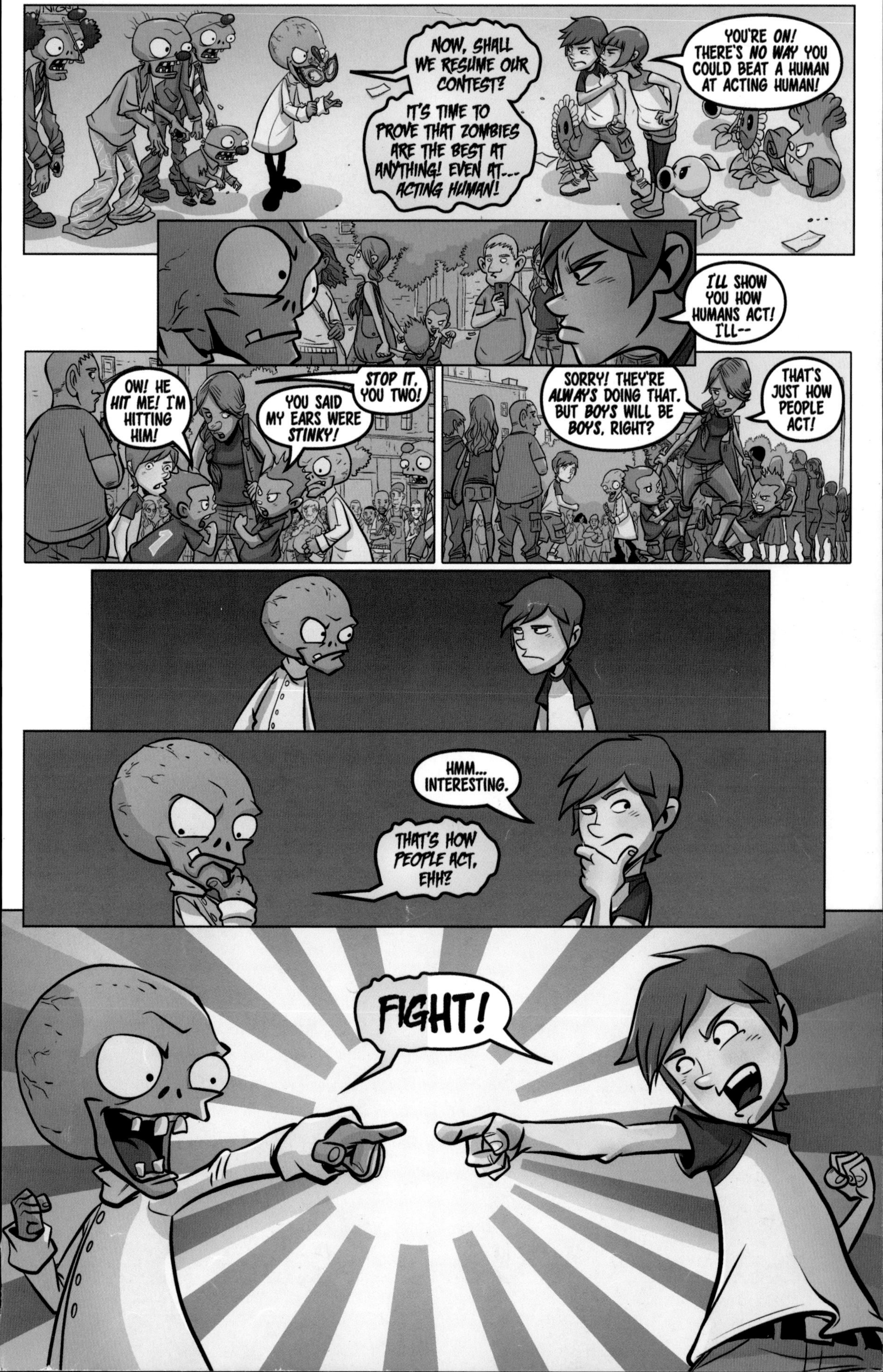
NOW, SHALL WE RESUME OUR CONTEST?
IT'S TIME TO PROVE THAT ZOMBIES ARE THE BEST AT ANYTHING! EVEN AT... ACTING HUMAN!
YOU'RE ON! THERE'S NO WAY YOU COULD BEAT A HUMAN AT ACTING HUMAN!
I'LL SHOW YOU HOW HUMANS ACT! I'LL--
OW! HE HIT ME! I'M HITTING HIM!
STOP IT, YOU TWO!
YOU SAID MY EARS WERE STINKY!
SORRY! THEY'RE ALWAYS DOING THAT. BUT BOYS WILL BE BOYS, RIGHT?
THAT'S JUST HOW PEOPLE ACT!
HMM... INTERESTING.
THAT'S HOW PEOPLE ACT, EHH?
FIGHT!

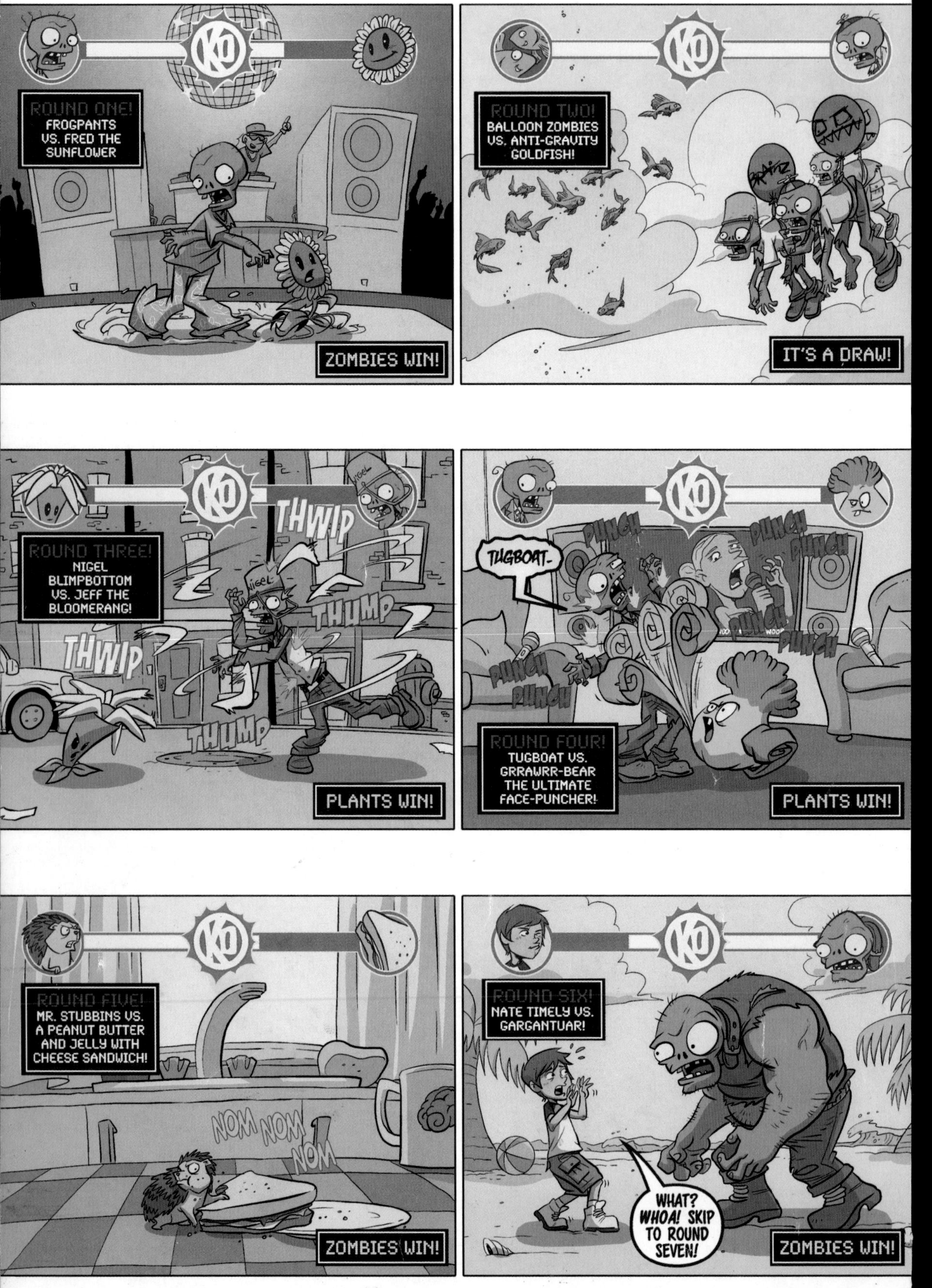

KO
ROUND ONE!
FROGPANTS VS. FRED THE SUNFLOWER
ZOMBIES WIN!
KO
ROUND TWO!
BALLOON ZOMBIES VS. ANTI-GRAVITY GOLDFISH!
BRAINZ
IT'S A DRAW!
KO
ROUND THREE!
NIGEL BLIMPBOTTOM VS. JEFF THE BLOOMERANG!
NIGEL
THWIP
THWIP
THUMP
THUMP
PLANTS WIN!
KO
TUGBOAT-
PUNCH
PUNCH
PUNCH
PUNCH
PUNCH
PUNCH
PUNCH
ROUND FOUR!
TUGBOAT VS. GRRAWRR-BEAR THE ULTIMATE FACE-PUNCHER!
PLANTS WIN!
KO
ROUND FIVE!
MR. STUBBINS VS. A PEANUT BUTTER AND JELLY WITH CHEESE SANDWICH!
NOM NOM NOM
ZOMBIES WIN!
KO
ROUND SIX!
NATE TIMELY VS. GARGANTUAR!
WHAT? WHOA! SKIP TO ROUND SEVEN!
ZOMBIES WIN!

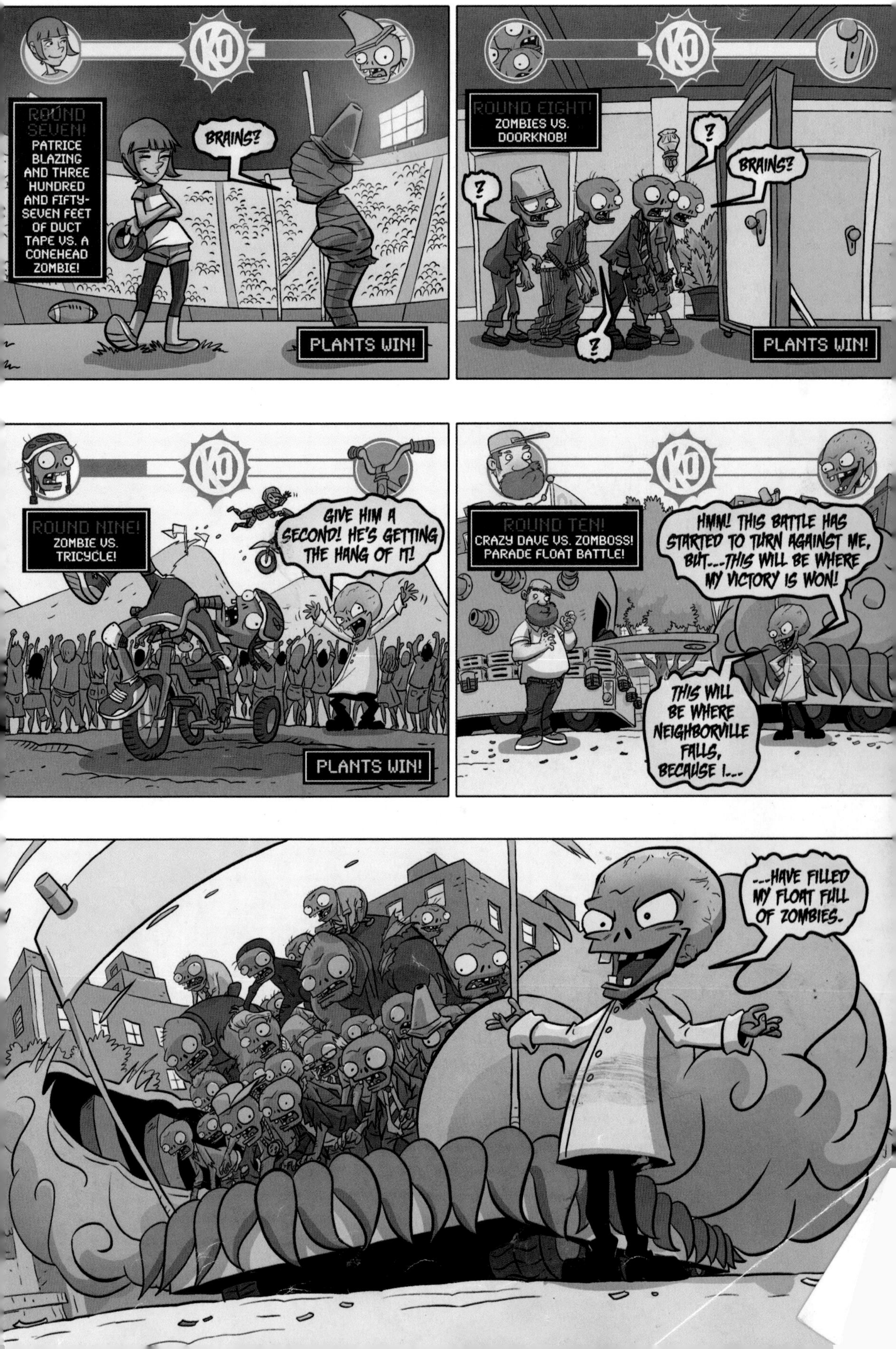
ROUND SEVEN! PATRICE BLAZING AND THREE HUNDRED AND FIFTY-SEVEN FEET OF DUCT TAPE VS. A CONEHEAD ZOMBIE!
BRAINS?
PLANTS WIN!
ROUND EIGHT! ZOMBIES VS. DOORKNOB!
BRAINS?
PLANTS WIN!
ROUND NINE! ZOMBIE VS. TRICYCLE!
GIVE HIM A SECOND! HE'S GETTING THE HANG OF IT!
PLANTS WIN!
ROUND TEN! CRAZY DAVE VS. ZOMBOSS! PARADE FLOAT BATTLE!
HMM! THIS BATTLE HAS STARTED TO TURN AGAINST ME, BUT...THIS WILL BE WHERE MY VICTORY IS WON!
THIS WILL BE WHERE NEIGHBORVILLE FALLS, BECAUSE I...
...HAVE FILLED MY FLOAT FULL OF ZOMBIES.

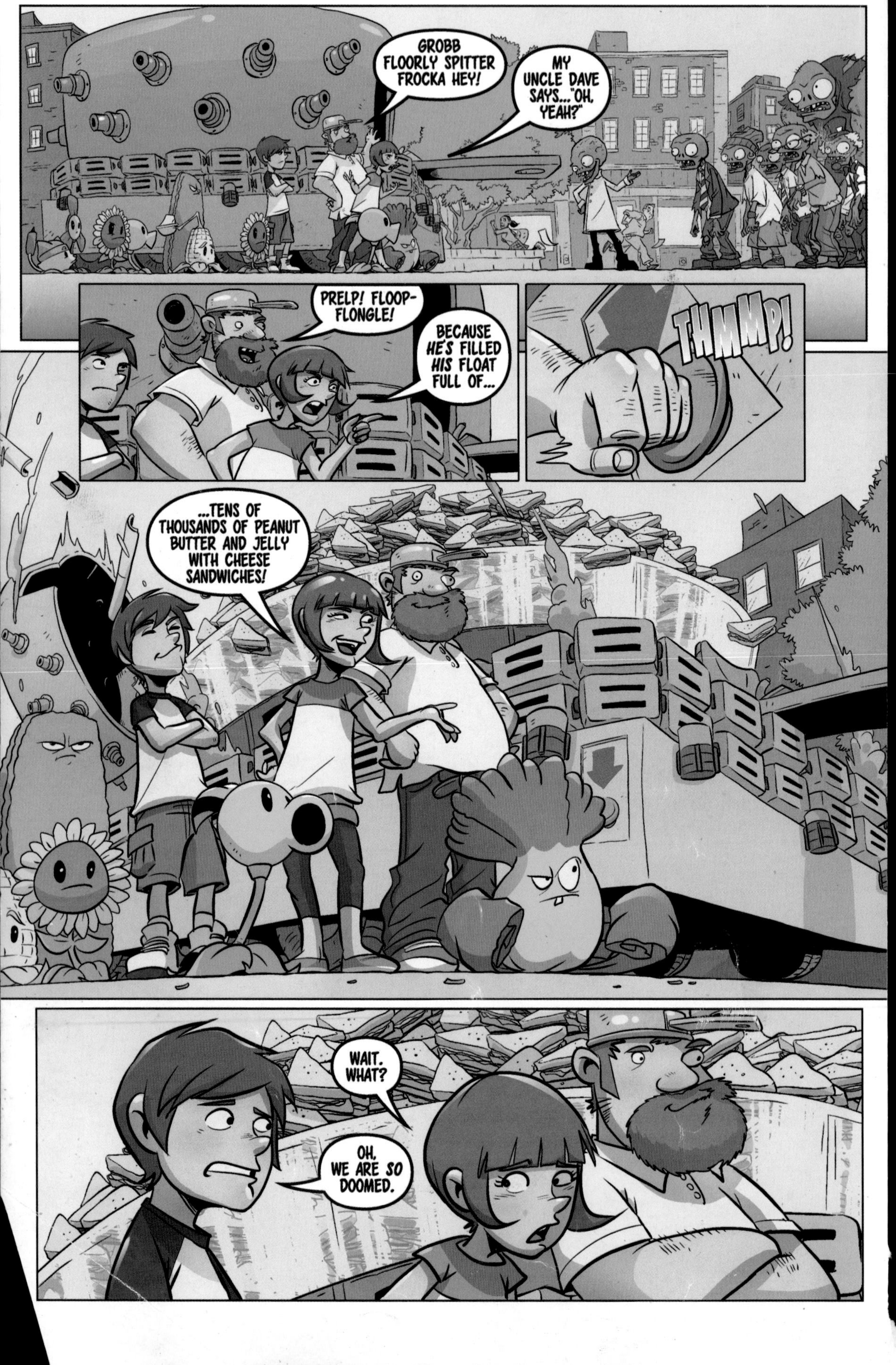
GROBB FLOORLY SPITTER FROCKA HEY!
MY UNCLE DAVE SAYS..."OH, YEAH?"
PRELP! FLOOP-FLONGLE!
BECAUSE HE'S FILLED HIS FLOAT FULL OF...
THMMP!
...TENS OF THOUSANDS OF PEANUT BUTTER AND JELLY WITH CHEESE SANDWICHES!
WAIT. WHAT?
OH, WE ARE SO DOOMED.

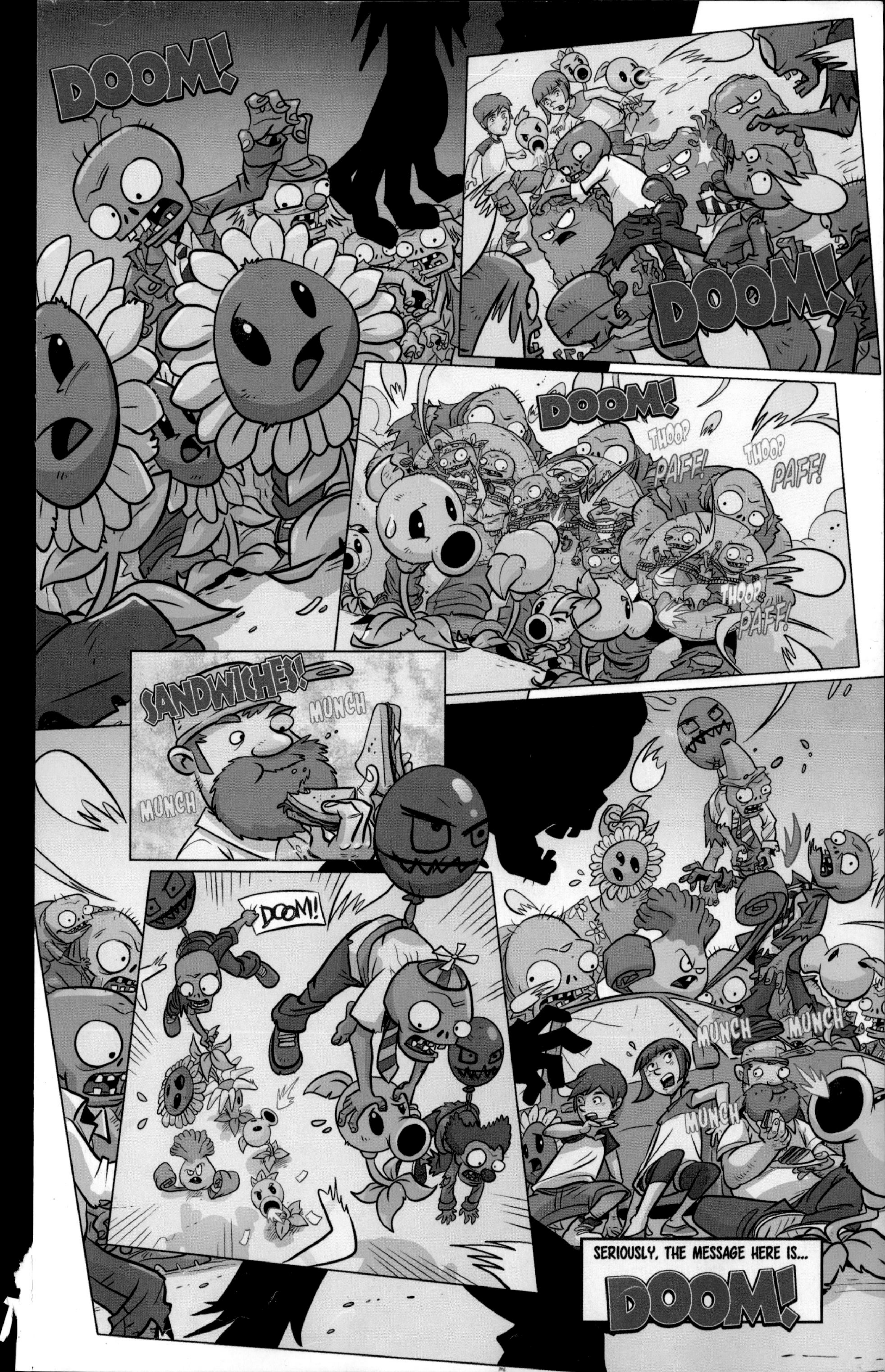
DOOM!
DOOM!
DOOM!
THOOP
PAFF!
THOOP
PAFF!
THOOP
PAFF!
SANDWICHES!
MUNCH
MUNCH
DOOM!
MUNCH
MUNCH
MUNCH
SERIOUSLY, THE MESSAGE HERE IS...
DOOM!

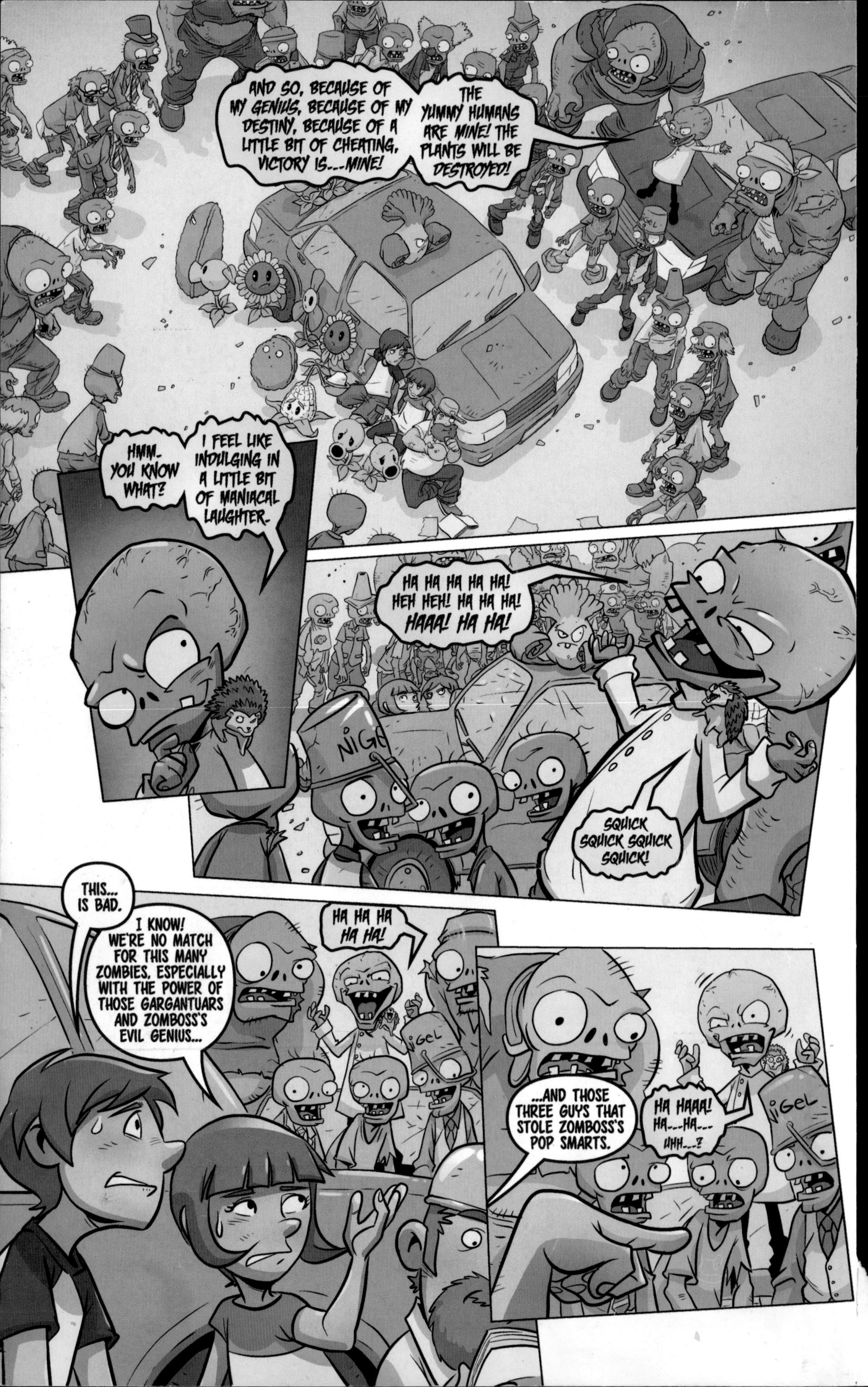
AND SO, BECAUSE OF MY GENIUS, BECAUSE OF MY DESTINY, BECAUSE OF A LITTLE BIT OF CHEATING, VICTORY IS...MINE!
THE YUMMY HUMANS ARE MINE! THE PLANTS WILL BE DESTROYED!
HMM. YOU KNOW WHAT?
I FEEL LIKE INDULGING IN A LITTLE BIT OF MANIACAL LAUGHTER.
HA HA HA HA HA! HEH HEH! HA HA HA! HAAA! HA HA!
SQUICK SQUICK SQUICK SQUICK!
THIS... IS BAD.
I KNOW! WE'RE NO MATCH FOR THIS MANY ZOMBIES, ESPECIALLY WITH THE POWER OF THOSE GARGANTUARS AND ZOMBOSS'S EVIL GENIUS...
HA HA HA HA HA!
...AND THOSE THREE GUYS THAT STOLE ZOMBOSS'S POP SMARTS.
HA HAAA! HA...HA... UHH...?

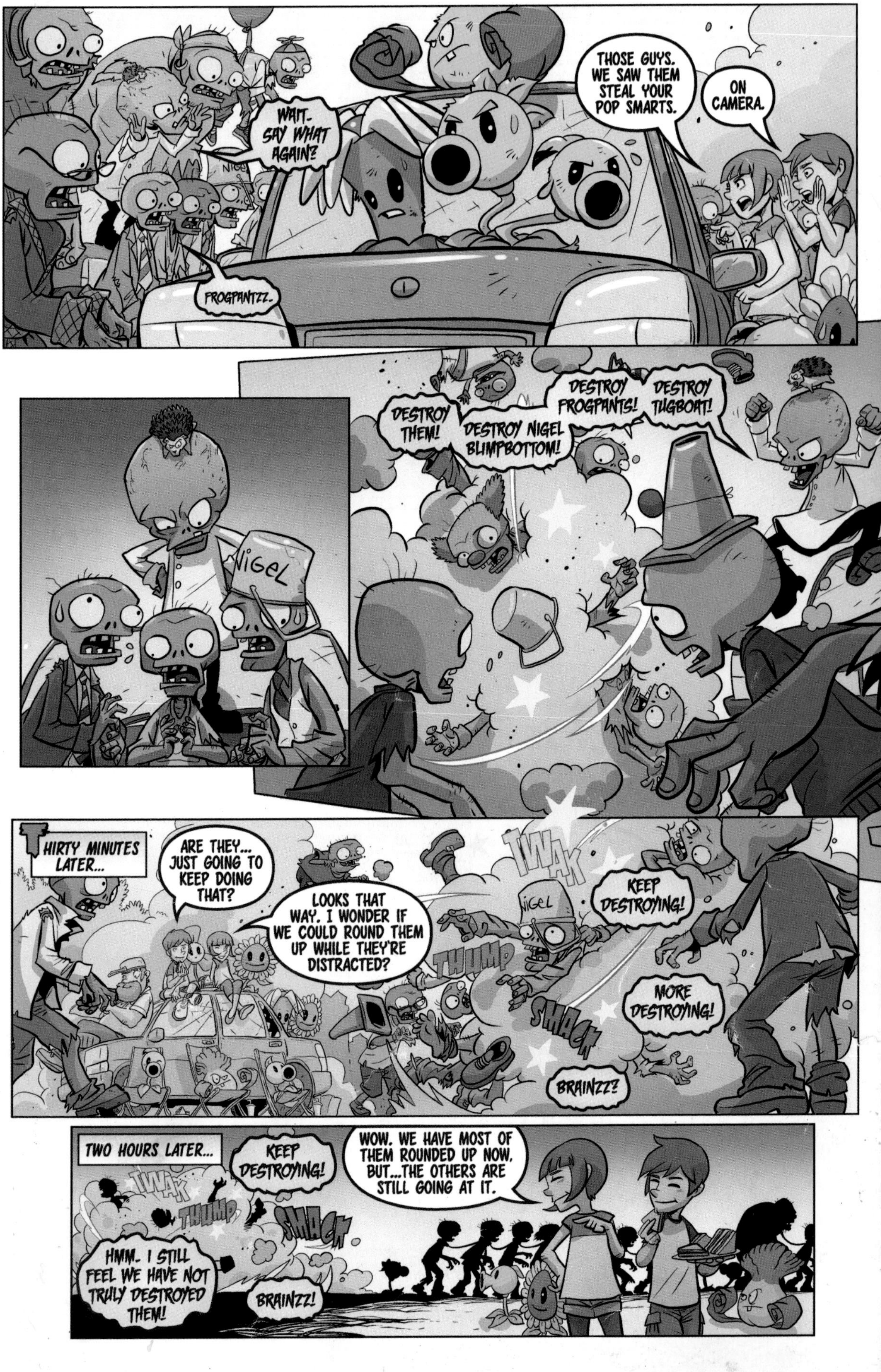

WAIT. SAY WHAT AGAIN?
THOSE GUYS. WE SAW THEM STEAL YOUR POP SMARTS.
ON CAMERA.
FROGPANTZZ.
DESTROY THEM!
DESTROY NIGEL BLIMPBOTTOM!
DESTROY FROGPANTS!
DESTROY TUGBOAT!
NIGEL
THIRTY MINUTES LATER...
ARE THEY... JUST GOING TO KEEP DOING THAT?
LOOKS THAT WAY. I WONDER IF WE COULD ROUND THEM UP WHILE THEY'RE DISTRACTED?
TWAK
KEEP DESTROYING!
NIGEL
THUMP
SMACK
MORE DESTROYING!
BRAINZZ?
TWO HOURS LATER...
KEEP DESTROYING!
WOW. WE HAVE MOST OF THEM ROUNDED UP NOW, BUT...THE OTHERS ARE STILL GOING AT IT.
TWAK
THUMP
SMACK
HMM. I STILL FEEL WE HAVE NOT TRULY DESTROYED THEM!
BRAINZZ!

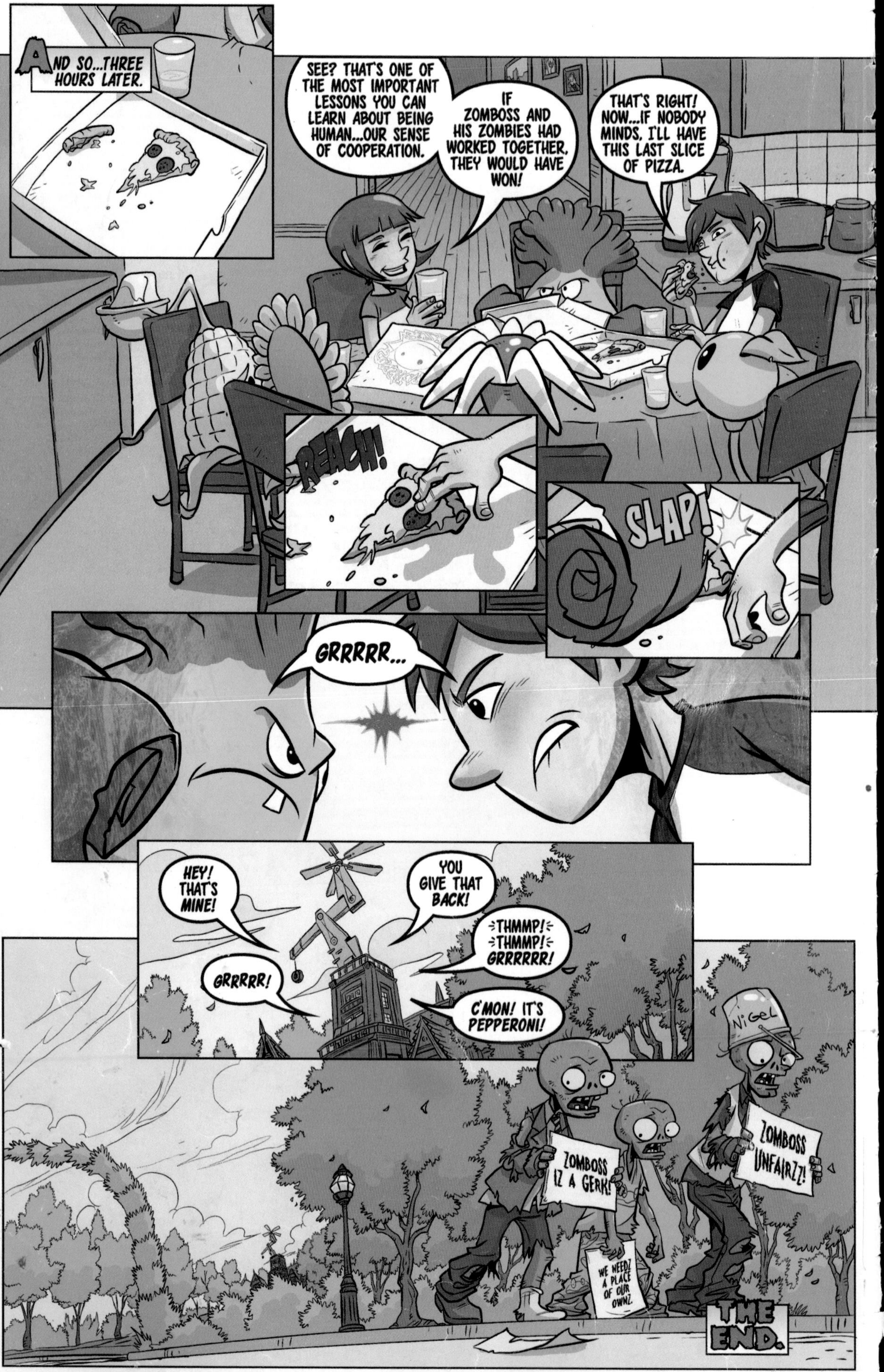
AND SO...THREE HOURS LATER.
SEE? THAT'S ONE OF THE MOST IMPORTANT LESSONS YOU CAN LEARN ABOUT BEING HUMAN...OUR SENSE OF COOPERATION.
IF ZOMBOSS AND HIS ZOMBIES HAD WORKED TOGETHER, THEY WOULD HAVE WON!
THAT'S RIGHT! NOW...IF NOBODY MINDS, I'LL HAVE THIS LAST SLICE OF PIZZA.
REACH!
SLAP!
GRRRRR...
HEY! THAT'S MINE!
YOU GIVE THAT BACK!
THMMP! THMMP! GRRRRRR!
GRRRRR!
C'MON! IT'S PEPPERONI!
NiGEL
ZOMBOSS IZ A GERK!
ZOMBOSS UNFAIRZZ!
WE NEEDZ A PLACE OF OUR OWNZ.
THE END.